The Roundhouse Cat

OZZIE'S
NEW ADVENTURES

The Roundhouse Cat

OZZIE'S
NEW ADVENTURES

by Lorenz Schrenk

Illustrated by Margarita Sikorskaia

BEAVER'S
POND
PRESS

Edited by Angela Wiechmann
Illustrated by Margarita Sikorskaia

ISBN 13: 978-1-59298-697-2

Library of Congress Catalog Number: 2016912102

Printed in the United States of America
First Printing: 2017
21   20   19   18   17   5   4   3   2   1

Cover and interior design by James Monroe Design, LLC.

Beaver's Pond Press, Inc.
7108 Ohms Lane
Edina, MN 55439–2129
(952) 829-8818
www.BeaversPondPress.com

To order, visit www.ItascaBooks.com or call (800) 901-3480.
Reseller discounts available.

CONTENTS

A SHORT INTRODUCTION

Several years ago, a wandering cat crept under the back fence of the old Jackson Street Roundhouse museum in Saint Paul, Minnesota. Museum volunteers fed him and took care of him. The name on his collar was Ozymandias, but the museum people called him Ozzie.

Ozzie liked the roundhouse and the workers there. He stayed and soon became a regular part of the museum. He helped by keeping mice and other animals away.

This is the second book in the series featuring stories about Ozzie's adventures. The stories may be fictional, but the settings and railroad descriptions are authentic.

1

OZZIE AND THE TURNTABLE PIT

It was a Monday. The roundhouse museum was closed. No volunteers were around. Ozzie headed out to check the rail yard. The sky was cloudy and overcast.

Ozzie spotted several birds near some trees. It was his job to chase away any birds, mice, or other intruders. So Ozzie hunched down. Quietly, he crept toward the birds. Just as he neared them, they spotted him. With beating wings and cries of alarm, they flew away.

Ozzie patrolled the yard to the rear fence. Then he headed back toward the roundhouse. Up ahead was the turntable pit.

The pit was a big round hole in the ground. Inside, the hole was lined with a cement wall. A steel turntable bridge crossed the pit. The bridge could be turned to line up with any track inside the roundhouse. Then an engine or car could be moved into the roundhouse.

Ozzie could hear birds chattering inside the pit. He crept to the edge and peered down. Below him, on the concrete floor of the pit, were five noisy birds. The birds did not notice Ozzie. If he leaped down, maybe he could catch one.

Ozzie jumped! About six feet down he flew. His tail stood up straight to guide his descent. His feet braced to stop his fall.

The sudden appearance of a cat scared the birds! Their wings flapped in panic. Ozzie lunged at one bird but caught only a few feathers. The frightened birds screeched as they rose out of the pit. They flew to the nearby trees. The birds hopped up and down among the branches and chirped nasty things to Ozzie.

Ozzie looked around. He suddenly realized he didn't know how to get back out. He saw no steps. He found no ramp. What should he do?

Maybe he could jump. Ozzie was a good jumper. He could leap from the floor to the top of the refrigerator.

Ozzie moved his head from side to side to judge the height of the wall. He crouched down, then sprang upward. Up, up he flew . . . but not quite high enough! Ozzie fell back down. With a quick twist of his body and flick of his tail, he landed on his feet.

Ozzie would have to jump higher. So he crouched again, even lower than before. Then he jumped! He soared upward. He tried to grab the top of the wall with his claws, but they slipped. Ozzie fell back down. This time, the hard concrete stung his feet and jolted his legs. It hurt.

No, he could not jump out. The wall was too high. He saw no way to climb out either. There seemed to be no escape!

Ozzie tried calling for help in a loud, sad voice. "Mreow! Mreowww!" It meant, "Come help me!"

But no one came. No one was at the roundhouse on Mondays. Maybe someone would show up in a day . . . or two . . . or three!

Meanwhile, the sky was getting darker. A drop of rain hit Ozzie's nose. He jerked his head back and sneezed. Another drop tickled his ear. Then more drops

came down, splattering on the concrete floor. Ozzie curled up in a small nook in the side of the pit. At least he was out of the rain.

It was cold that night. By morning, Ozzie was chilled and hungry. He was an unhappy cat! The rain had stopped, but the floor of the pit was still wet.

Once again, Ozzie called loudly for help. "Mmrrrow! Mmrrroww!"

Still, no one came. Occasionally, birds flew by. Their calls seemed to make fun of him!

After waiting for two or three hours, Ozzie started searching again for a way out. He walked around the turntable pit. He looked at the turntable from one end to the other. Then he noticed a short metal rod about two feet above the floor. It was about one foot long. There were four rods above it to make five rods in total. They were fastened near the bottom of a tall steel post. The post was part of the big steel arch that crossed the center of the turntable.

What were the rods for? Maybe a determined cat could climb the rods like a ladder. Ozzie was a good climber!

Ozzie stretched up on his hind feet and reached as high as he could for the first rod. He hooked a paw over it. He pulled himself up, then curled his other front paw over the rod. For a few seconds, he hung there.

The rod was still wet from the rain. Carefully, Ozzie managed to get one of his back feet onto the slick rod. It was difficult, but he kept his balance. Then he pulled up his other back foot.

There he was, perched with all four feet on the first rod. But there were four more rods above him on this strange, slippery ladder.

Ozzie reached a paw up to the next rod. Suddenly, he slipped! He fell to the floor again.

Maybe this climb was too hard. Should he wait for someone to come pull him out? If so, he might be trapped there for days. No, he would try again!

Ozzie reached for the first rod. He slowly pulled himself back up. Then he wrapped a paw over the second rod. Moving carefully, he crawled on top of it. Ozzie looked up. Three more rods to climb on this slippery ladder!

Ozzie hooked a paw over the third rod and pulled himself up. Two more rods to go!

He hauled himself up on the fourth rod. One more rod to go! But he was getting tired.

Ozzie wrapped a paw over the top rod. He started to

crawl his way onto the wet rod. But then he slipped! He almost fell!

Would he be too tired to make it to the top?

Straining with effort, Ozzie pulled himself onto the top rod. Success! He balanced there for a moment. Then he reached across to the wood walkway. He dug his claws into the closest board and dragged himself over. He was finally out of the turntable pit!

Ozzie was exhausted. Not dog-tired but cat-tired! Walking slowly, he headed for the roundhouse. He made his way back to his home in the crew office. He lapped up some water, crawled onto his bed, and fell asleep. He did not wake up until hours later.

Maybe that would be the last time Ozzie jumped down without knowing how to get back up!

2

OZZIE AND THE
MERRY-GO-ROUND

One day, Jim opened the door to the round-house crew office and said, "Come along, Ozzie. Let's go buy a leash for you. That way, you can go more places."

Being a cat, Ozzie may have not understood what that meant. He followed Jim anyway. He liked going places with Jim.

"We're going to a pet store," Jim explained. "Kirsten and Jennie will go with us."

Ozzie's ears perked up. Kirsten and her daughter, Jennie, were two of his best friends at the roundhouse.

Jennie rode in back with Ozzie. She petted him. He rubbed his cheek against her hand.

"Oh, Ozzie, you're so cute!"

Ozzie purred in response.

"Look, Ozzie. I've got a new ball," said Jennie. She held out a small red ball with yellow stripes. "I got it for my birthday."

Ozzie knew about balls. Before living at the round-house, Ozzie had other owners. They used to roll a ball to him. He would crouch down and pounce on it. If the ball rolled away, he would chase it and pounce again. That was before they moved away and left him on the street.

Several times during the ride, Ozzie reached out a paw to bat at the ball. But Jennie always held it tightly.

As they drove, Kirsten suggested, "Maybe after we buy Ozzie's new leash, we can stop at Como Park to try it out. The park has lots of space where we can take Ozzie for a walk. He won't be able to visit the big zoo there or the conservatory with its beautiful flowers and plants. But Como Park still has a lot of things to see and do. I like to hike around the lake or watch people playing baseball or soccer. I also like the miniature golf course."

"That's a good idea," agreed Jim. "Ozzie could use the exercise."

"Can we ride the merry-go-round too?" Jennie asked. "That's one of my favorite things!"

"We can, but Ozzie will have to wait outside, of

course," Kirsten answered. "Sorry, Ozzie."

When they reached the pet store, Jim said to Ozzie, "We should put you into your carrier bag now."

Ozzie's tail swished back and forth. He did not like the carrier. But he let Jim put him in so they could all go into the store.

Inside, Jim told the salesperson, "We need a leash for our cat."

The woman pointed to a display rack with cat leashes. "You'll need a six-foot leash to walk your pet in the parks. Let me see if his collar has a loop."

She started to reach inside the carrier. Ozzie growled. He did not like strangers reaching for his neck.

Kirsten spoke softly, "It's okay, Ozzie. We just need to see if we can attach a leash to your collar. That way, we don't have to keep you in the carrier bag all the time."

Ozzie finally let Kirsten check his collar.

Ozzie's friends bought a black leather leash, then returned to Jim's car.

"I'm glad that's done," said Jim. "Now, let's head to Como Park."

At the park, Ozzie and his friends trotted along a path. Ozzie had no trouble walking with the leash. Sometimes, though, he didn't always want to go the same direction as the others. Then Jim would give him a gentle tug on the leash.

After a while, they stopped at a bench to catch their breath.

Jennie showed Ozzie her ball. "Here, Ozzie," she said as she tossed it a few feet away.

Still on the leash, Ozzie ran and pounced on it. Each time Jennie threw the ball, Ozzie went after it.

"Let's head over to the merry-go-round," Jim said.

Soon they heard the cheerful sound of carousel music. As they neared, they could see people riding on brightly painted wood horses. The horses moved up and down as they circled around.

Kirsten and Jennie bought tickets. Jim stayed with Ozzie outside the building. When the merry-go-round stopped, Kirsten climbed onto a dappled gray horse. Jennie, still clutching her new ball, climbed onto a horse with an alligator carved on its side.

The merry-go-round started up. The music played, and the painted horses went up and down as the carousel turned.

"Look at us!" the two happy riders called out as they went by.

The merry-go-round finally slowed and stopped. Kirsten and Jennie climbed down from their horses. Just then, the ball slipped out of Jennie's hand. The ball hit the edge of the platform, then bounded toward the low fence.

"My ball!" she cried out.

The ball struck a post and bounced back. It rolled underneath the merry-go-round. Jim saw the ball, but he was helpless to stop it. Ozzie saw it too, his head popping up.

Jennie's face showed her dismay. Kirsten bent down and looked under the merry-go-round. She could see the ball, but it was out of reach.

"Jennie, it's too far under for me to get."

Tears welled up in Jennie's eyes.

Jennie ran over to the man who operated the merry-go-round. She explained what had happened.

"I'll try to get it," the operator said. He brought over a short broom the staff used to sweep up popcorn and candy wrappers. Unfortunately, the broom could not reach the ball either.

"I'm sorry," he said. "I don't know what else we can do. I have to start the next ride."

As the merry-go-round started up again, tears streamed down Jennie's face. She might never see her ball again.

Then Jim had an idea. He looked down at Ozzie.

"Maybe when the merry-go-round stops, Ozzie could crawl underneath and bat the ball out."

Ozzie's ears twitched at his name.

Jim went to tell the operator his plan.

"Okay," the operator said. "But you'll have to be quick!"

The merry-go-round stopped, and riders climbed off. Jim set Ozzie down near the spot where the ball had rolled.

Jim said, "Get the ball, Ozzie. Get the ball!"

Maybe Ozzie understood him or maybe not. Either way, Ozzie did spot the red-and-yellow ball just a few feet away beneath the merry-go-round. He crawled under and went after it. He batted the ball until it rolled out from beneath the platform.

Ozzie's friends cheered. So did some people standing in line who saw Ozzie's rescue.

Jennie stooped down, pulled Ozzie toward her, and gave him a big kiss. He was her hero!

Ozzie wiggled a bit. But he seemed to understand

he had made her happy. And he seemed to understand he had done something others could not do. He held his tail high.

Back at the roundhouse, Ozzie's friends rewarded him with extra snacks.

Carolyn, at age four, inspired this story when she asked Granddad to write about Ozzie and a merry-go-round.

3

OZZIE RIDES THE STEAMBOAT

One summer afternoon, Jim walked up to Ozzie and asked, "Ozzie, would you like to ride the steamboat?"

Ozzie did not understand. What was a steamboat? Why was Jim going to see it? Would this be a new adventure? Ozzie, always curious, followed Jim to his car and jumped in.

As Jim drove, he explained, "The steamboat used to be part of the railroad museum. The boat is now on a big lake to the west. It's a long drive from our roundhouse. Some of my old friends help run the steamboat. They've invited us to go for a ride."

When Ozzie and Jim reached the lake, Jim opened the door. Ozzie climbed down.

"Should we use your leash?" Jim asked.

Ozzie backed away.

"Okay," said Jim with a laugh. "Just stay close to me, then. Let's go see the steamboat."

Ozzie followed Jim down a path toward the big blue lake. A sea gull stood in the grass nearby. What an easy target! Ozzie charged toward the bird. With a loud flapping of wings, the sea gull rose into the air. Then the big bird turned around and dove toward Ozzie, screeching loudly. The surprised cat scampered back toward Jim.

The gull's cries attracted two other gulls. All three then swooped toward Ozzie.

"Now see what you've done!" yelled Jim. Waving his cap, he chased the birds away.

Ozzie stayed close to Jim as they continued down to a pier. They could hear the slow "slap, slap, slap" of small waves hitting the beach.

When Jim stepped onto the pier, Ozzie hesitated. He did not care much for water.

"Come along, Ozzie," said Jim. "People are waiting for us."

Ozzie stepped uneasily onto the pier. Through the gaps in the wood planks, he could see the water shining and rippling underneath.

Just then, a fish jumped out of the water with a loud "SPLASH!" The sound startled Ozzie. He turned to run back to shore.

"It's okay, Ozzie," Jim said. "The fish won't bite you."

Ozzie did not seem convinced.

Out on the lake, they saw boats. Some were tied to buoys. Others made loud whining sounds as they sped by. Still other boats glided along quietly, moved by the breeze in their sails.

Soon they came to a large yellow boat with big glass windows. The boat also had a tall yellow smokestack. A big red banner with white letters flapped in the breeze. The name *Minnehaha* marked the front end of the boat. Of course, the name was something Ozzie, being a cat, could not read. But Jim could!

The *Minnehaha* was a real steamboat. The steam engine had a slow, rhythmic pattern. The boiler gave off a steady "shhhhhhhhhhh" of steam. There was also a slight "hissssss" as wisps of steam escaped from the engine.

Jim's friend Curt waited by the boat. He was the captain. He greeted Jim and Ozzie with a cheerful, "Hello! Welcome aboard." Captain Curt wore a neat uniform with a white shirt and a black cap. His cap had a silver badge with the name *Minnehaha* on it. He bent

down and petted Ozzie. "Hello, Ozzie," he said.

Jim stepped onto the steamboat. Ozzie eyed the gap between the pier and the boat. He also eyed the water below. Perhaps it would be better to chase small birds back in the parking lot . . .

Jim reached down and lifted Ozzie onto the boat. "Come on, Ozzie," said Jim. "We're going for a ride."

Ozzie watched as a member of the steamboat's crew unfastened the ropes that held the *Minnehaha* to the dock. He pushed the boat out from the pier, then jumped onto the deck. As he pulled the rope up, one end splashed in the water. He coiled the rope up on the deck, where it left a small puddle.

A very loud, long "whooooooooooop" came from the *Minnehaha's* whistle. It hurt Ozzie's ears. Next, a small bell rang. "Ding-ding, ding-ding!" The steamboat began backing away from the pier. The deck quivered slightly. The bell sounded again. One "ding-ding" to stop, then another "ding-ding" to change direction. The steamboat headed out into the lake.

The engine bell rang three times: "ding-ding, ding-ding, ding-ding." The engine sped up. The *Minnehaha* slowly cut through the waves, up and down.

Ozzie shifted uncomfortably with the movement

beneath his paws. Gradually, he grew more used to the motion. He began enjoying the rhythmic rise and fall of the boat. He moved to the rear deck and relaxed in the warmth of the sun.

After a while, Ozzie stood up and stretched. He looked at the steam engine. It sat in the open center of the boat. A member of the crew sat beside the engine.

"Hello, kitty," she said, rubbing his neck.
Ozzie purred.

Ozzie walked to the front of the boat. This was a good place to stand. The wind tickled his fur in a pleasant way. He sniffed the lake smells. The only annoyance was an occasional splash of water from an extra-large wave.

Suddenly, a large fish jumped up nearby. Ozzie turned. Fish were natural objects of interest to a cat. Another fish erupted from the water. Then yet another fish leaped up very close to the *Minnehaha*.

Ozzie jumped to get a better view. He landed right in the puddle left by the wet rope!

Ozzie skidded across the wet, slippery deck. His tail whipped back and forth. His feet hit the wood strip at the edge of the deck. His feet stopped, but he didn't! He flipped over the side.

"SPLASH!"

Ozzie was in the lake!

One of the crew members saw what happened. He shouted, "Man overboard—I mean, cat overboard! Port side!"

Jim came rushing to the side of the deck. He could only watch as the crew immediately started the man-overboard drill.

The engineer stopped the propeller. One crew member dropped a life ring floatation device into the water near Ozzie. Another crewmember brought a long pole with a hook, ready to grab Ozzie. He kept close watch on the cat.

Ozzie's paws peddled furiously as though he were trying to climb out of the water. The steamboat drifted ahead.

Ozzie was mad. He did not like water, did not like the sudden dunking, and did not like having done such a silly thing as slip off the boat. But there he was, dog-paddling. No. More correctly, he was *cat*-paddling! Anyway, he was swimming. Fortunately, cats naturally know how to swim.

The *Minnehaha* continued to slide past Ozzie. The stern of the steamboat was close to Ozzie when a big hand reached down and plucked the wet cat out of the water. Back on the steamboat deck, water dripped from Ozzie and pooled beneath him.

Someone brought a thick towel and began rubbing the water from Ozzie's coat. Now that Ozzie was safe, Jim almost laughed at how upset and miserable Ozzie appeared.

By the time the *Minnehaha* returned to the pier, Ozzie was almost completely dry.

Ozzie stayed close to Jim as they walked back to the car.

"Well, Ozzie," said Jim, "I guess you won't need a bath this week!"

Ozzie didn't seem to find Jim's comment funny!

4

OZZIE GOES TO SCHOOL

 zzie was almost always well behaved. Of course, there were times when his cat instincts took over. That could create problems. Something like that happened the time he was invited to visit a school.

"Ozzie," Jim said one day, "would you like to go with me to visit some children at their school? I'm going there to tell them about the roundhouse. I want them to know about all the things they can see and do here."

Ozzie didn't know anything about schools. But he was always glad to have a new adventure.

Once they arrived at the school, Jim snapped Ozzie's leash onto his collar before opening the car door. "Mrs. Peterson is expecting us," he said. "She told me her students are very excited about meeting a genuine round-house cat!"

Ozzie looked up at Jim and meowed.

Ozzie was on his best behavior as he and Jim walked into the school office. Miss Henderson, the school secretary, was there. She led them down the hall to Mrs. Peterson's room.

"Children, let's welcome Jim and Ozzie the roundhouse cat," Mrs. Peterson said. "Jim will tell you all about the roundhouse. Ozzie lives there. He helps greet visitors. He also helps keep unwanted birds and mice away."

"Thank you for inviting us," said Jim. "We're glad for the chance to come and meet you."

Ozzie's ears twitched when he saw all the boys and girls looking at him with friendly curiosity.

"The roundhouse, where Ozzie lives, was built over one hundred years ago to take care of steam locomotives of the Great Northern Railway," Jim said. "These locomotives pulled trains to places like Chicago, Duluth, and Fargo. The trains came back every day with mail, food, and people. I'll bet some of you have family members who worked for a railroad."

The children listened intently as Jim continued.

"Steam locomotives required lots of care, so the people at the roundhouse were busy. But some years ago, diesel-electric locomotives replaced steam locomotives.

The diesels required less maintenance and the railroad no longer needed the roundhouse. Now it's been turned into a railroad museum. It has many things for you to see and do. You even can take a short caboose ride. You also can arrange to have birthday parties there in an old passenger car. It can be a lot of fun!"

The children clapped with excitement.

"Now, if you'd like to get a closer look at Ozzie, maybe two or three of you at a time can come up front. If you are very gentle, you can pet him."

The children started coming up in small groups to meet Ozzie. Ozzie accepted their touches without complaint. He was so quiet and good that Jim unfastened his leash. Ozzie even greeted some of the children with a friendly "Meow."

One girl asked, "What does Ozzie mean when he meows like that?"

"We don't always know," Jim answered. "For some reason, cats usually meow to people but not to other cats. A meow may mean 'hello' or 'feed me' or 'pet me' or 'play

27

with me.' If we pay close attention, we can sometimes figure out what he's telling us."

When one boy acted a little too rough, Ozzie arched his back and made a snarling sound. Jim explained, "And that's how Ozzie says, 'I don't like that. Back off!'"

As she petted Ozzie, one girl asked, "Does he have a motor inside?"

"No, of course not," Jim said. "Why do you ask?"

"Well, he makes a sound like a motor when I pet him. It even feels like he has a motor inside."

"Oh!" said Jim with a laugh. "Ozzie is purring. He's telling you he feels happy. He must really like how you're rubbing his back."

The children treated Ozzie gently. They petted him and spoke nicely to him. They asked Jim where Ozzie slept, what food he ate, and how he got his name. They also asked about the roundhouse.

"Is it really round?" one boy asked.

"It's partly round," answered Jim. "That's so tracks can run into it from a turntable outside. The tracks then spread out inside the roundhouse like fingers on an open hand."

Just as Jim started to explain more about the round-house, Ozzie's head perked up. He had spotted a goldfish swimming in a small tank on a bookcase. He took a step toward the bookcase.

"No, Ozzie," Jim commanded in a sharp voice. "You leave that fish alone!"

Ozzie stopped. He looked up at Jim as though to say, "Who, me? You didn't really think I was going after that fish, did you?" Then Ozzie turned away from Jim as though he had been insulted.

The time for Ozzie's visit in the classroom was coming to an end. Jim was relieved that Ozzie had listened to him and ignored the fish. He was proud of Ozzie.

Just then, Ozzie's head perked up again. He saw something move in the cage sitting on the table at the front of the room. A small wire wheel inside the cage was turning in circles. Ozzie looked closer. Something was running inside the wheel. It was a gerbil!

Ozzie had never seen a gerbil before. As far as he was concerned, it was a mouse. And his job was to catch mice.

Ozzie leaped onto the table. He landed on the teacher's lesson plans, scattering them in every direction. He also tipped over a vase of flowers. Ozzie jumped toward the gerbil and knocked his cage over.

Some children shrieked with surprise, others with excitement.

Both Jim and Mrs. Peterson rushed to halt the disaster. Jim ran toward Ozzie. Mrs. Peterson ran to the table.

The frightened gerbil huddled in the corner of its overturned cage. Meanwhile, water from the flower vase spread across the table. It soaked Mrs. Peterson's papers and dripped to the floor. Mrs. Peterson tried to stop the flood, rescue her papers, and calm the gerbil all at once. She didn't succeed at any of her efforts.

Jim reached out to grab Ozzie. Just then, Ozzie decided it was time to leave. He didn't like the water spreading across the floor. So he scampered up the aisle between the rows of desks, much to the delight of the children. Some laughed. One boy shouted, "Go, Ozzie!" And other students sat stunned.

Jim chased after Ozzie. He cornered him and grabbed him up. All the while, Jim alternated between yelling at Ozzie and apologizing to Mrs. Peterson.

With a very quick good-bye, the two visitors made their way out of the school. Ozzie was firmly fastened to his leash.

Mrs. Peterson was left to dry out her papers, pick up the flowers, and wipe up the floor. The students didn't calm down for the rest of the day. And the gerbil never

31

fully recovered from its unexpected fright. From that day forward, it was hesitant to run in its exercise wheel.

For his part, Jim never again took Ozzie to visit a school classroom. Maybe that's why Ozzie never learned to read or write.

5

OZZIE AND THE PUMPKIN TRAIN

One beautiful October morning, Jim walked into the roundhouse.

"Hello, Ozzie," he said. "Today I'm going to Osceola, Wisconsin, to help with the Pumpkin Train. Want to come along? It's our last train of the season there."

Ozzie liked going places with Jim (except perhaps to see the veterinarian). Ozzie had visited Osceola many times. Museum volunteers ran trains there during the summer. The Pumpkin Train was a favorite event. It came just before Halloween. People could ride the train to the next town and enjoy special activities there. They especially liked searching the pumpkin patch for the perfect pumpkin to take home.

During the drive to Osceola, Jim said, "Ozzie Cat, I'll be a car attendant today. First I'll help passengers board the train at Osceola. Then I'll ride with them to Dresser. That's the next station. It won't be a long ride. When we get to Dresser, I'll help passengers off the train. There will be a lot going on in Dresser," Jim added in a serious tone. "I don't want you to wander off! Stay close to the depot."

Ozzie may not have been listening. In fact, he seemed to be napping.

When they reached Osceola, a train with a big green locomotive and four passenger cars was sitting at the station. Ozzie's favorite car, the A-11, was part of the train. He liked it because it had tables with lots of food.

It was a lovely day. The trees were brilliantly colored—gold and red and shades of brown. A few birds swooped overhead. People were waiting on the platform. Some even wore Halloween costumes.

The train conductor was there. He wore a dark-blue uniform and a cap with a shiny "Conductor" badge. He greeted passengers and answered their questions.

After checking his watch one more time, the conductor blew his whistle. "All abooaaaard!" he called out.

Jim helped passengers climb onto the train. Then he

lifted Ozzie onto the A-11 car.

The engineer in the green locomotive blew two shrill blasts on the air horn. "HREEEP! HREEEP!" The train was about to start. With a slight jerk, the cars began to move.

As the train rolled along, Ozzie wandered among the passengers. Many people petted him. He enjoyed that. Some people took pictures of him.

The conductor came into the car. "The next stop will be Dresser," he announced. "Everybody off for the pumpkin patch!"

The train slowed to a stop. One more "HREEEP!" sounded. That meant the engineer had set the brakes. It was now safe to get off the train.

Jim helped passengers step down to the platform. Ozzie tried to avoid being stepped on. Then he too jumped down to the platform. After everyone departed, the train slowly backed away from the station.

"Remember what I said, Ozzie. Don't wander away," said Jim. "Stay nearby."

However, Ozzie was not always a good listener. How could he just stay in one place? The Dresser station was a busy place!

Many people were coming and going. There was

a yellow depot with a small railroad museum and
Halloween displays. Next to the depot stood colorful
plastic tents. They contained inflated bouncy castles.
The castles shook wildly from children jumping up and
down inside.

Nearby was a shelter for games. There were tables
and activities everywhere. One game was a beanbag toss.
Ozzie didn't care much for that. It would be too easy for
some excited child to step on him or throw a beanbag his
way! And Ozzie definitely didn't like the face-painting
at the next table. At a birthday party back at the roundhouse, someone had once tried to paint him!

Across the tracks was a grassy area with picnic tables
surrounded by trees and bushes. Ozzie started to walk
across the tracks.

"Look out!" someone yelled.

Two teenaged boys came speeding down the track on
a handcar. They almost hit him! Ozzie jumped out of the
way just in time.

People were eating picnic lunches at wood tables.
Ozzie walked over and meowed to coax them into giving
him bits of food.

After eating his snacks, Ozzie explored the other
attractions. However, he stayed away from the fire pit,

where people were roasting hot dogs and marshmallows. Hot marshmallows and cat fur was not a good combination!

Beyond the fire pit was a field with bales of hay. The bales had been arranged into a puzzle maze for children. Next, Ozzie saw a fenced-in area with orange pumpkins scattered around. The pumpkins were ready to be taken home and carved into jack-o'-lanterns. People went from pumpkin to pumpkin searching for one that looked just right.

Suddenly, Ozzie stopped. Something deep in the tall grass had moved! What was it?

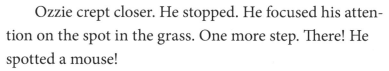

Ozzie watched the spot. His ears stood alert.

Something moved again!

Ozzie crept closer. He stopped. He focused his attention on the spot in the grass. One more step. There! He spotted a mouse!

Ozzie sprang!

But the mouse had heard Ozzie. It darted away. Ozzie missed!

Ozzie chased the mouse. Whenever Ozzie got close, the mouse ran or jumped away. Ozzie was quick, but so was the mouse. Ozzie followed the mouse deeper into the weeds—and farther and farther from the depot.

Just then, Jim returned to the platform. That was where he had told Ozzie to stay.

Jim looked around. He called out, "Ozzie! Ozzie!"

The cat didn't come.

Next, Jim looked inside the depot. No cat there! He looked in the bouncy castles. Not there either. Jim talked to the people at the picnic tables. They remembered seeing Ozzie, but they didn't know where he had gone.

The train returned to the depot. The stationmaster announced, "Hello, folks. It's time to get back on the train. It will leave in ten minutes."

Jim helped people climb onto the train. Many carried bags with pumpkins. Even as he helped passengers, he kept his eyes open for Ozzie. But there was no sign of the missing cat.

Should Jim go hunting for Ozzie? However, his job was to keep passengers safe during their train trip. He had to stay with them.

The train's horn sounded. "HREEEP! HREEEEP!"

From deep in the tall grass, Ozzie heard the two

blasts. He had lived at the roundhouse long enough to know what those sounds meant. The train was about to leave! He was supposed to be on that train!

He raced as fast as he could back toward the station. He arrived there just as the last car rolled away. He ran after the train, but he was too late!

He had been left behind. Even his friend Jim was gone. Had he abandoned Ozzie? Would Ozzie ever get back home?

What should he do? He could wait at the depot in case the train came back. But would it?

Perhaps he could follow the track back to Osceola. But it was a long way to walk. It would be dark before he got there. And what if the track split into two directions? He might go the wrong way. Ozzie was brave and resourceful, but he was, after all, a city cat. He didn't know much about this area out in the country.

All the lonely cat could do was wait!

Then a car drove up to the depot. A door slammed. There came Jim around the corner! Ozzie ran toward him.

"Ozzie, where have you been?" Jim exclaimed.

Ozzie, being a cat, couldn't say. But Jim didn't really need an answer. He was just glad he had found Ozzie.

Ozzie seemed to feel the same way. He rubbed against Jim's legs and purred.

It's good to have a friend who comes when you need him!

6

OZZIE AT CHRISTMASTIME

"Good morning, Ozzie," said Jim, as he opened the office door.

Ozzie gave a soft "Meow" in reply.

"This will be a busy day," said Jim.

"Christmas at the roundhouse is a popular event. There will be plenty of people for you to meet."

Ozzie seemed to understand.

They stepped through the door into the museum lobby. Visitors were already lined up on the ramp to the ticket counter.

"Now behave yourself, Ozzie," Jim said. "I'm going out to the caboose. You stay in here." Jim turned and headed for the back door.

Ozzie looked at the big, freshly cut evergreen tree

standing near the ticket area. Two museum volunteers, Tom and his son Billy, were hanging decorations on the branches.

"Hello, Ozzie," Billy said. "What do you think of our Christmas tree? Isn't it great?"

Like many cats, Ozzie loved to climb. He often crawled up in trees so he could look around and perhaps catch a careless bird.

This Christmas tree was filled with brightly colored objects. Lights shined in various colors. Many shiny balls were scattered among the branches. There were also some toylike birds with multicolored feathers. A white angel topped the tree.

When Tom and Billy weren't looking, Ozzie crawled underneath the tree. He began climbing up among the branches and decorations.

He almost bumped into a large, shiny red ball. On the ball was a strange round-faced cat! Ozzie didn't realize it was his own reflection. He reached up to push the "other cat" away.

The red ball bounced down through the branches. It hit the

floor and broke with a loud "Pop!" Small pieces of red glass scattered across the floor.

Tom came running. "What happened?" he cried out.

Ozzie scrambled down. He headed straight for the table where volunteers served popcorn and hot chocolate. He avoided the table where children were having their faces painted with blue-and-silver snowflakes. Someone had once tried to paint him!

Then a loudspeaker announced, "Santa Claus and Mrs. Claus will be arriving on Track 1 at the rear of the roundhouse."

Visitors hurried toward the door. Ozzie crawled under a display case to avoid the trampling feet. Then he followed everyone from a safe distance.

A white caboose rolled into view from behind the rail yard's steel shed. A black switch engine pushed the caboose. Santa and Mrs. Claus stood on the rear platform of the caboose. They were dressed in red with white fur trim. They waved to the waiting crowd.

With screeching brakes, the caboose slowed to a stop. Santa and Mrs. Claus stepped down.

"Merry Christmas!" they said to everyone.

Ozzie went back into the museum to get out of the cold. He stopped at a table where children were making

Christmas cards. His friend Kirsten was helping them.

"Hello, Ozzie," she said. She reached down and stroked his head.

Ozzie rubbed against her ankles. Kirsten was a favorite friend.

Nearby, three musicians played Christmas carols. "Good King Wenceslas looked out . . ." they sang as they played.

One musician played a guitar. The second musician pushed and pulled a stretchy box. The box also had a keyboard. Ozzie had never seen or heard an accordion before.

The third musician played a silver drum. The beat of the drum was strong. Ozzie swung his tail back and forth, keeping time like a bandleader's baton.

Suddenly, Ozzie's tail stopped. He looked at the drummer. What kind of creature was this? It wasn't a person. It wasn't like anything Ozzie had ever seen! It had a face like a frog's. Dark glasses hid its eyes. It wore a red cap with fur trim. Its red-gloved hands moved drumsticks in time with the accordion player's foot.

This drummer was too strange for comfort! Ozzie did not understand it was a mechanical puppet connected to the accordion player's foot. Ozzie turned

46

and walked away.

Ozzie next went to a table set up with a Lego train. Just then, Ozzie caught a glimpse of a small figure disappearing into a tunnel at the far end of the track. Had he just spotted a mouse?

Ozzie jumped onto the table. He crouched down in front of the tunnel. Sooner or later, that mouse would have to come out. And when it did, Ozzie would pounce!

Ozzie was so busy watching the tunnel that he didn't hear a toy handcar rolling quietly down the track behind him. On the car was a toy mouse. It had circled around and was coming directly behind Ozzie. It ran right into him!

The surprised cat leaped high in reaction to the mouse's sneak attack!

A volunteer saw Ozzie. "Hey! Get off of there!" he yelled.

Ozzie scampered away to the old wood coach car in the back corner. No one was in the car.

A Christmas tree stood in one corner of the car. This tree was smaller than the one by the entrance ramp. Brightly colored ornaments sparkled in this tree too. Strings of shiny tinsel decorated the branches. A large silver star shone at the top.

Ozzie looked at the tree. Then he looked around. No one was there to stop him this time. He began climbing.

On his way up, he brushed against an ornament. It swung but stayed in place. Climbing higher, Ozzie bumped another ornament. This one swayed for a moment, then fell. The ornament bounced down through the branches and landed on the floor. Luckily, it did not break.

Ozzie continued his climb. He was near the top when the branch under him suddenly snapped. Ozzie fell!

Ozzie tried to keep his balance and stop his fall. He twisted this way and that. He grabbed with his front paws and pedaled with his rear paws. He flicked his tail. But nothing worked! He half-fell, half-scrambled from branch to branch on his way down.

More ornaments came loose. They bounced down through the branches. The first one broke with a crash, followed by another, and then more. Bits of broken glass littered the floor.

Kirsten came running. She took one look at Ozzie and yelled, "What are you doing? Get out of there!"

Ozzie could not stop until he reached the floor. A string of green tinsel encircled his neck. Red tinsel wrapped around his leg. It trailed behind him.

Ozzie stumbled away, tripping over the tinsel as he ran. He was such a comical sight that nearby visitors began laughing.

Even Kirsten laughed. "Oh, Ozzie, you're so funny! Hang on," she said. "Let me help you."

Ozzie stopped. Kirsten walked over, bent down, and carefully removed the decorations.

"Ozzie, you don't have to dress up like a Christmas tree," she said. "We already have two. Now go and try to stay out of trouble."

Ozzie crept over to a display cabinet. He curled up underneath and napped!

SOME RAILROAD WORDS

Beanery. An eating house or café.

Big hole. To make an emergency stop of a train.

Big hook. The derrick used to lift locomotives or railroad cars.

Conductor. The person in charge of a train and its crew.

Cornfield meet. A head-on collision between two trains.

Deadheading. Moving an empty train or car.

Drover car. A coach car, usually old, used by cowboys travelling with cars of livestock.

Engineer. The person who runs a locomotive.

Fireman. The person who feeds coal or fuel oil to a locomotive so it can run.

Frog. A heavy piece of metal at the center of a track switch. It has grooves for railroad wheels.

Hobo. A person who hitches rides on trains and is willing to work; may be an abbreviation of "homeward bound."

Hoghead. Slang for a locomotive engineer.

Hotshot. A train with orders to run fast and with priority over other trains.

Lightning slinger. Slang for a telegraph operator.

Locomotive. A unit used to pull or push a train. Some use steam power, some use diesel-electric power, and some use electrical power.

Outlawed. A train or crew member forbidden to operate because of some defect or because of reaching the limit of hours allowed on duty.

Railroad yard. A place with multiple tracks for storing or switching railroad cars.

Reefer. Slang for a refrigerator car.

Roundhouse. A building where locomotives are housed and serviced, usually built around a turntable.

Spur. A track that branches off another track and comes to a dead end.

Wig-wag. An old type of lighted signal that swings back and forth to warn automobiles of an approaching train.

ACKNOWLEDGMENTS

With special appreciation to . . .

Ann, my wife of many years, who allowed a pesky fictional cat to stay in our home.

Our children—Janet, Stephen, and Lisa—and our grandchildren—Charles, Elizabeth, Carolyn, and Josephine—who endured my bedtime storytelling and asked for more.

The crew at Beaver's Pond Press, who turned my writing into real books suitable for polite company of all ages.

Editor Angela Wiechmann and artist Margarita Sikorskaia, who merit special mention for their invaluable help.

My fellow members of the Society of Children's Book Writers and Illustrators group in north suburban St. Paul. With persistence, they labored long and hard to shape me into something resembling a children's book author.

The Minnesota Transportation Museum, which provided a home for Ozzie for some years and whose members offered ideas and assistance for this book project.

Ann Merriman and her husband, Christopher Olson, who cared for Ozzie after he retired from active museum work.

Joy and Gary Wildung and Jasper, technical advisors on feline behaviors.

ABOUT THE AUTHOR

The author and his wife reside in the Twin Cities area of Minnesota. The Ozzie series had their origin in bedtime stories told to their three children and four grandchildren.

The author is a retired research scientist and manager and a railroad historian. He has degrees from The George Washington University and from The Ohio State University. He served in the U.S. Navy during the war in Korea and later helped start one of the first Montessori schools in Minnesota. He has co-authored five volumes on the history of the Northern Pacific Railway and written many shorter articles.

He especially enjoys creating stories that both entertain and help to educate children.